The Sky's The Limit

PRAISE FOR *STORYSHARES*

"One of the brightest innovators and game-changers in the education industry."
– Forbes

"Your success in applying research-validated practices to promote literacy serves as a valuable model for other organizations seeking to create evidence-based literacy programs."

- Library of Congress

"We need powerful social and educational innovation, and Storyshares is breaking new ground. The organization addresses critical problems facing our students and teachers. I am excited about the strategies it brings to the collective work of making sure every student has an equal chance in life."
– Teach For America

"Around the world, this is one of the up-and-coming trailblazers changing the landscape of literacy and education."
- International Literacy Association

"It's the perfect idea. There's really nothing like this. I mean wow, this will be a wonderful experience for young people."   - Andrea Davis Pinkney, Executive Director, Scholastic

"Reading for meaning opens opportunities for a lifetime of learning. Providing emerging readers with engaging texts that are designed to offer both challenges and support for each individual will improve their lives for years to come. Storyshares is a wonderful start."
- David Rose, Co-founder of CAST & UDL

The Sky's The Limit

Kimberly Le Bel

STORYSHARES

Story Share, Inc.
New York. Boston. Philadelphia

Storyshares
Story Share, Inc.
24 N. Bryn Mawr Avenue #340
Bryn Mawr, PA 19010-3304
www.storyshares.org

Inspiring reading with a new kind of book.

Interest Level: Middle School
Grade Level Equivalent: 4.7

9798885978460

Book design by Storyshares

Printed in the United States of America

Storyshares Presents

1

I can remember the struggles I went through starting as far back as elementary school. That's when I was labeled "L.D." In case you don't know, that stands for "learning disabled."

It was in third grade that this label was stamped on my forehead. It's a label that has stayed with me ever since.

I sailed right through nursery school. It seemed pretty easy to me.

Riding tricycles. Looking out the window. Sitting at the table having a quick snack and drinking apple juice.

I did some exploring while digging in the sandbox. I felt the sand run through my fingers.

I also learned about water. Measuring and pouring, using different measuring cups. The water would trickle down through a funnel and onto the water wheel.

I even learned how to count in Chinese.

The sky was the limit. There were so many things to learn.

I couldn't believe just how fun learning new things had become.

In kindergarten, there was more playing, riding bikes, snack time, and meeting new friends.

Friends who would be with me through this journey for the next twelve years. We were also learning how to tie our shoes—something I remember not being able to do.

2

By the third grade, things seemed to change. Work became harder. I realized I was struggling with one of my class assignments.

The assignment was to do research on an animal. Write down as much information as I could on index cards. Then present it in front of the class.

Writing in pencil, you could see where I had used an eraser over and over again. I had to get rid of so many mistakes.

There were so many mistakes because I didn't know what words to use.

Writing sentences was very difficult for me. I knew what I wanted to say. But I could not write it down so that my teacher could understand. I became so frustrated.

The eraser marks were soon red marker from my teacher. Lines and lines of red, showing where I had made errors. Where I needed improvement.

Sadly, this was just the beginning of many mistakes that I would make throughout school.

It wasn't just a change in my academic ability. There was also a change in who I was becoming.

It was clear to me that I was different. All my friends were finding it out as well.

Before third grade, there were no groups to classify what reading level you were in. In third grade, there were groups. They classified us.

I was now separated from my friends. I was placed in the lowest level possible.

My friends that I had been with since nursery school were all academically smarter than me.

We were now separated, because of my IQ. Something I had no control over.

3

Because I was having a hard time with my classes, I couldn't wait for recess.

Outside there weren't any reading groups or labels. I was free!

That is until the teasing started on the playground.

One time my so-called friends approached me during recess. They asked me if I wanted to join their club.

I remember answering them with excitement in my voice, "Yes, please let me be in your club."

But it wasn't going to be that easy. I had to earn it.

My classmates surrounded me, making me feel trapped. It was then that I heard someone say, "In order for you to be cool like us and be in our club, you have to tell us the times table."

Having always struggled with math, I was unable to give them the correct answers.

Laughter soon filled the air as the group of girls left. As they walked away, they told me I was too stupid to be in their club.

I don't know how I got through it. I was holding back tears. I was all alone outside, away from my teachers.

I could see the school in the distance, a place that I felt safe in. But it was far away.

Somehow, I managed to get through the rest of the day.

But then I had to ride on the same school bus with the same girls that teased me earlier on the playground.

4

Once I reached home, I would run into my mother's arms in tears. I would tell her how badly I was treated in school that day.

The teasing continued throughout the school year. Sometimes every day.

I was teased for not knowing how to tell time.

Not knowing how to ride a bicycle.

Not knowing how to swim.

Having learning disabilities, I had no concept of time or space.

My math and reading skills were horrible.

I felt I spent most of my time trying to catch up with everyone else.

For me, it was exhausting! Physically, mentally, and emotionally.

5

In the evenings after dinner, I would sit at the kitchen table with my parents. They would help me complete my homework.

I would have many meltdowns because I didn't know what I was doing. I was also easily distracted.

I was also jealous that my brother and sister finished their homework. They could go watch T.V. in the other room.

There were many tears and feelings of doubt. I would say I can't do this.

I don't know the answer.

I hate school.

My teachers don't like me.

I'm stupid.

I was just so sick to my stomach.

6

When I was in middle school, I continued to struggle with friendships and academics. But now, I also struggled with low self-esteem.

I was placed in special education classes. Classes that were very small and were made up mostly of boys. For that reason alone, I disliked school.

I was, however, in some mainstream classes. English was one of them.

In English class we were going over our spelling words preparing for the Spelling Bee Contest for our school.

There was a group of us that stood in the front of the class, reciting the correct spelling of a word we were given.

I noticed that slowly, one by one, my classmates were asked to sit back down at their desks. They had misspelled the word.

I was in shock. How were they getting these words wrong?

The words were easy. So easy. Even I knew how to spell them.

Before I knew it, it was just me and one other classmate standing in front of the class.

There we were shoulder to shoulder, like in a duel. The last one standing would be the winner! The best speller in the class!

The word rolled off my teacher's tongue and entered my brain. I kept repeating the word over and over in my head until I spelled the word out loud so everyone could hear.

Next it was my classmate's turn. And then the unthinkable happened. I won! It was me!

There I was standing in front of everyone. I was shocked that I beat all of the smart kids in my mainstream class!

The sky's the limit!

My teacher congratulated me and told me how proud she was.

Except I soon found out the whole thing was just a trick.

The Sky's The Limit

7

My classmates, of course, knew all the words. They just pretended they didn't know how to spell.

The winner of the class spelling bee would go on to the school-wide spelling bee. My classmates didn't want to have to stand in front of the whole school.

They all thought the spelling bee contest was stupid and for losers. They wanted nothing to do with it.

Neither did I.

I ended up speaking in private with my teacher after class.

I begged her not to make me stand up on stage in front of everyone. Begged her to not make me make a fool out of myself again.

It was bad enough that I was just humiliated in front of the class. I could only imagine what it would be like being embarrassed in front of the whole middle school.

8

In high school, things seemed to only get worse. Classes became bigger. The work became even harder.

Each day I attended resource room. Resource room is where kids with what's now called "special education needs" get put for one class every day.

We were supposed to be given extra help. Or taught basic lessons. But mostly it meant that we were different.

I was embarrassed that resource room was part of my class schedule.

I also had learning specialists that met with me weekly. The specialist would come to my school on different days of the week and pull me out of my mainstream classes.

She would actually knock on the classroom door and let my teacher—as well as all of my classmates—know that she was there to meet with me.

It was a huge embarrassment. Everyone would stare at me as I packed up my books and walked out the classroom.

As we went down the hall to the library, I sometimes would walk slower or faster. Anything to make sure we were not right next to each other.

I know, real mature. But I really didn't want to be seen with her.

Once we reached the library, I requested we sit at a table all the way in the back. That way no one I knew would see me.

9

I think what upset me the most about seeing these specialists was that they would pull me out of a class I was having difficulty in.

They would arrive in the middle of a lesson or project to meet with me so we could work on reading comprehension. But it was during math class. One of my worst subjects.

I didn't need to be working on my reading comprehension right then. I needed to be working with my teacher and the other students in math class.

Without fail, later in the day, my classmates would approach me. They would ask me who that lady was who took me out of class.

I could feel my face turning red. With the sound of panic in my voice, I would quickly answer, "Oh I just had to meet with her about something."

I would change the subject and walk away before they would figure out why I had left class.

10

In my junior year of high school, my guidance counselor wanted to discuss colleges.

We sat in his office. He had my student file lying open on his desk. He looked up at me.

Without hesitation, he told me I may want to look into getting a job when I get out of high school.

The way my grades were looking, he wasn't sure if college was for me.

I was heartbroken and ashamed. I felt I let my parents down. I felt I even let myself down.

But he was right.

It all made sense somehow. How could someone like me get into college?

My parents received school progress notes every year. They said exactly what the guidance counselor was saying.

"Shows weakness in vocabulary work."

"Needs to improve reading comprehension, work is inconsistent."

"Needs to use time more effectively, lacks confidence in ability."

"Needs to develop more independence in work habits."

One of my favorite progress notes came from my physical education class: "Sometimes comes to class without necessary materials/preparation."

It was gym class for crying out loud.

11

In January of my senior year, the committee on special education had a meeting with my mom. They wanted to reevaluate the services they were offering because I was impaired in speech and language.

The meeting took place because I was refusing to meet with my speech and language specialist two times a week. You remember the lady that would take me out of class and humiliate me? Yes, that's the one.

As a result of this meeting, speech and language was dropped from my curriculum. I felt like I had accomplished something.

As strange as this may sound, it was the first time ever that I felt like an adult.

I had spoken up and fought against something that I felt wasn't right. And someone out there heard my cry for help.

I wasn't getting anything out of meeting with this specialist. I was only being humiliated, which only made me angry.

Knowing that I would no longer be meeting with her, I felt my self-esteem improving.

However, I was told that I still needed to attend resource room four times a week for forty-five minutes.

I wasn't too thrilled about it in the beginning. But it was towards the end of the school year and graduation was quickly approaching.

It was probably one of the most important classes I would take.

I used those four days out of the week in the resource room to work on my senior paper.

Every student needed to hand in their senior paper in order to graduate.

And graduate is what I did!

12

After summer, I attended a two-year community college. I found out about this college from a substitute teacher.

At that time, not many colleges had a support system for students with learning disabilities. So, she thought this one was worth looking into.

When I graduated from high school, things were very different.

The internet had not yet been developed. There were no online support systems to help me with my academics. There was no easy way to research colleges.

My mom called the community college to make an appointment for me to meet with their Learning Disabilities Specialist.

Within a few days, my parents and I made the three-and-a-half-hour car ride to look at the college and its on campus housing.

Before I knew it, I was enrolled to attend college there in the fall. The community college was a blessing.

I was receiving not only academic support, but emotional support as well.

13

Being so far away from home and the very small community I grew up in, I became very homesick.

Because of this, the Learning Disabilities Specialist took me under her wing. This was a hard part of my journey. And she got me through it.

I don't know if she knew it at the time, but besides my mother, she was my best friend. She was my only friend away from home.

My two years at the community college went by quickly. I graduated with an associate's degree in Early Childhood/Nursery Education.

After graduating, I kept in touch with the Learning Disabilities Specialist with phone calls and letters. I also took the three-and-a-half-hour ride back to the college to see her.

Today, it has been many years since we have spoken.

I do continue to think about her often and the impact she had on my life.

14

Soon after getting my associate's degree, I started attending college again. Because I was so homesick the first time, I decided to attend classes at a local college.

I was going for my bachelor's degree in Behavioral Science. I was lucky enough to still receive special services at the college.

I was also living at home with my parents, who had always been so supportive of me. I felt by living at home, I could really focus on my studies.

I completed many credits in my field of study. I also had a grade point average of 3.3.

I was now a member of both the International Honor Society in Social Sciences and the National Honor Society in Psychology.

Reaching these achievements made me think back to the day when I was sitting with my guidance counselor in high school. The man who didn't believe that I would even get into a college.

When someone tells you that you won't amount to anything, or your classmates are calling you stupid, you start to believe that of yourself.

Going through school has been one of the longest and toughest journeys of my life. There were many tears.

There were moments of doubt when I didn't believe that I would ever get through any of it.

Those evenings I was sitting at the kitchen table doing homework and having meltdown after meltdown were particularly hard.

I also look back at the tests and behavioral observations that were performed on me. Tests such as

Picture Completion and Arrangement, as well as Block Design and Object Assembly.

It was as if my brain were being picked apart as I took these tests.

The Sky's The Limit

15

I write this for any individual who has ever had doubt. Anyone who wants to give up. Who fears that they can't do anything because they are stupid.

I was that person so many times. Even to this day I struggle.

When I start to struggle and I'm feeling frustrated or having low self-esteem, I look back at all that I have achieved.

I try to remind myself that I can do anything, just as long as I set my mind to it.

The sky has no official beginning or end. There is no limit or boundary.

The sky's the limit!

About The Author

Kimberly Le Bel is a contributing author to the Storyshares library.